P9-CRL-986

This Book
Belongs To

MARC BROWN'S
PLAYTIME RHYMES

A Treasury for Families to Learn and Play Together

MARC BROWN'S
PLAYTIME RHYMES

A Treasury for Families to Learn and Play Together

LB

LITTLE, BROWN AND COMPANY
New York   Boston

Introduction

When my son Tucker was in nursery school, he became very engaged with finger rhymes, and of course, I did too. Finger rhymes became a favorite activity for us to share. Over the years, I have collected more than 350 finger rhymes, and I offer my very favorites here for new generations to enjoy.

This collection was gathered with the purpose of engaging and entertaining children and introducing them to poetry. I am indebted to the Flint Public Library in Flint, Michigan, for compiling an extensive collection of these rhymes. And I thank all the children, parents, teachers, and librarians who shared their favorite finger rhymes with me.

I would like to dedicate this book, and all the joy that went into making the art, to Mother Goose. From what I know, it was her son-in-law, Thomas Fleet of Pudding Lane in Boston, who collected her "melodies" and first published them in 1719. And we are all so grateful that he did.

R0440036168

Table of Contents

Whoops! Johnny

 Johnny,

 Johnny,

 Johnny,

 Johnny,

 Whoops!

 Johnny.

 Whoops!

 Johnny,

 Johnny,

 Johnny,

 Johnny.

 Now you do it.

(The trick is that most people forget
to cross their arms when they finish.)

6

7

The Counting Game

 One, two, buckle my shoe;

 Three, four, knock at the door;

 Five, six, pick up sticks;

 Seven, eight, stand up straight;

 Nine, ten, ring Big Ben;

 Eleven, twelve, dig and delve.

Do Your Ears Hang Low?

 Do your ears hang low?

 Do they wobble to and fro?

 Can you tie them in a knot?

 Can you tie them in a bow?

 Can you throw them over your shoulder

 Like a continental soldier?

 Do your ears hang low?

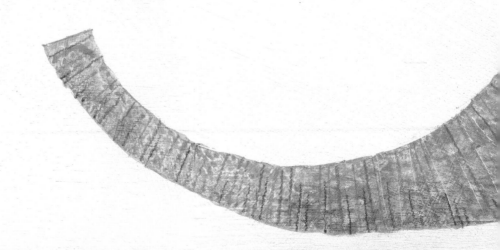

Teddy Bear

 Teddy Bear, Teddy Bear, turn around.

 Teddy Bear, Teddy Bear, touch the ground.

 Teddy Bear, Teddy Bear, show your shoe.

 Teddy Bear, Teddy Bear, that will do!

 Teddy Bear, Teddy Bear, go upstairs.

 Teddy Bear, Teddy Bear, say your prayers.

 Teddy Bear, Teddy Bear, turn off the light.

 Teddy Bear, Teddy Bear, say good night.

The Wheels on the Bus

 The wheels on the bus go round and round,

 Round and round, round and round.

 The wheels on the bus go round and round,

 All through the town.

The driver on the bus says, "Move on back,

 Move on back, move on back."

 The driver on the bus says, "Move on back,"

 All through the town.

 The children on the bus say, "Yak yak yak,

 Yak yak yak, yak yak yak."

 The children on the bus say, "Yak yak yak,"

 All through the town.

 The mommies on the bus say, "Shh shh shh,

 Shh shh shh, shh shh shh."

 The mommies on the bus say, "Shh shh shh,"

 All through the town.

I'm a Little Teapot

 I'm a little teapot, short and stout.

 Here is my handle.

 Here is my spout.

 When I start to steam up, hear me shout,

 "Tip me over and pour me out."

The Itsy Bitsy Spider

 The itsy bitsy spider

 Climbed up the waterspout.

 Down came the rain

 And washed the spider out.

 Out came the sun

 And dried up all the rain.

 So the itsy bitsy spider

 Climbed up the spout again.

Two Little Monkeys

 Two little monkeys jumping on the bed.

 One fell off and bumped his head.

 Mama called the doctor, and the doctor said,

 "No more monkeys jumping on the bed!"

Five Little Pigs

 This little pig went to market.

 This little pig stayed home.

 This little pig had roast beef.

 This little pig had none.

 This little pig cried, "Wee, wee, wee!"

 All the way home.

The Church

This is the church.

This is the steeple.

Open the doors

And see all the people!

Here Is the Beehive

 Here is the beehive. Where are the bees?

 Hidden away where nobody sees.

 Watch and you'll see them leave their little hive.

 One bee, two bees, three, four, five.

 Bzzzzzz...say the bees and all fly away!

HOME
SWEET
HIVE

Grammy's Glasses

 These are Grammy's glasses.

 This is Grammy's hat.

 This is the way she folds her hands

 And lays them in her lap.

Little Bunny

 There was a little bunny who lived in the wood.

 He wiggled his ears as a good bunny should.

 He hopped by a squirrel.

 He hopped by a tree.

 He hopped by a duck.

 And he wiggled by me.

 He stared at the squirrel.

 He peeked round the tree.

 He stared at the duck.

 But he winked at me!

Sleepy Fingers

 My fingers are so sleepy,

 It's time they went to bed.

 First you, Baby Finger,

 Tuck in your little head.

 Ring Man, now it's your turn.

 Then comes Tall Man Great.

 Pointer Finger, hurry, because it's getting late!

 Let's see if they're all cozy.

 No, there's one to come.

 Move over, Little Pointer,

 Make room for Master Thumb!

The Squirrel

Whisky, frisky, hippity-hop,

Up he goes to the treetop.

Whirly, twirly, round and round,

Down he scampers to the ground.

Furly, curly, what a tail—

Tall as a feather, broad as a sail!

Where's his supper? In his shell.

Snappity, crackity, out it fell.

There Was a Little Turtle

 There was a little turtle

 Who lived in a box.

 He swam in the puddles

 And climbed on the rocks.

 He snapped at the mosquito.

 He snapped at the flea.

 He snapped at the minnow.

 And he snapped at me.

 He caught the mosquito.

 He caught the flea.

 He caught the minnow,

 But he didn't catch me!

Five Little Goblins

 Five little goblins on a Halloween night

 Made a very, very spooky sight.

 The first one danced on her tippy-tip-toes.

 The next one tumbled and bumped his nose.

 The next one jumped high up in the air.

 The next one walked like a fuzzy bear.

 The next one sang a Halloween song.

 Five little goblins played the whole night long!

Snowflakes

 Merry little snowflakes

 Falling through the air,

 Resting on the steeple

 And tall trees everywhere,

 Topping roofs and fences,

 Capping every post,

 Covering the hillside where we like to coast.

 But when the bright spring sunshine

 Says it's come to stay,

 Those merry little snowflakes

 Quickly run away.

The Snowman

 Roll him and roll him until he is big.

 Roll him until he is fat as a pig.

 He has two eyes and a hat on his head.

 He'll stand there all night,

 While we go to bed.

My Book

 This is my book; it will open wide

 To show the pictures that are inside.

 This is my ball, so big and round,

 To toss in the air

 Or roll on the ground.

 Here's my umbrella to keep me dry

 When the raindrops fall from a cloudy sky.

 This is my kitty; just hear her purr

 When I pet her soft, warm fur.

47